CREEPY CREATURES

Edited By Lynsey Evans

First published in Great Britain in 2024 by:

Young Writers
Remus House
Coltsfoot Drive
Peterborough
PE2 9BF
Telephone: 01733 890066
Website: www.youngwriters.co.uk

FOREWORD

Welcome Reader!

Are you ready to discover weird and wonderful creatures that you'd never even dreamed of?

For Young Writers' latest competition we asked primary school pupils to create a creature of their own invention, and then write a mini saga about it - a hard task! However, they rose to the challenge magnificently and the result is this fantastic collection full of creepy critters and bizarre beasts!

Here at Young Writers our aim is to encourage creativity in children and to inspire a love of the written word, so it's great to get such an amazing response, with some absolutely fantastic stories.

Not only have these young authors created imaginative and inventive creatures, they've also crafted wonderful tales to showcase their creations. These stories are brimming with inspiration and cover a wide range of themes and emotions - from fun to fear and back again!

I'd like to congratulate all the young authors in this anthology, I hope this inspires them to continue with their creative writing.

CONTENTS

Ardeley St Lawrence CE (VA) Primary School, Ardeley

Tawana Sithole (10)	1
Annabelle York (7)	2
Annabelle Krieger (10)	3
Toby Ballard (8)	4
Grace Koop (8)	5
Hudson Streatfield (9)	6
Rogue Baker (8)	7
Chloe Wilkinson (9)	8

Avon House Preparatory School, Woodford Green

Adam Maniyar (8)	9
Dhilan Mistry (7)	10
Muhammad Aliyaah Atif (8)	11
Azrael Gale (8)	12
Theo Duncan (7)	13
Alanna Sarker-Islam (8)	14
Yusuf Zayaan (7)	15
Yorkshire Swarbrick (8)	16
Ethan Cai (7)	17
Amaya Randerwala (7)	18
Aarit Gandhi (7)	19
Xyla Bygrave (8)	20
Kaelan Kaelas (8)	21
Max Springett (8)	22
Jacob Srokowski (7)	23
Yusuf Ishfaq (8)	24
Aiden Bhandari (7)	25
Nia Biston (8)	26
Ezra B	27
Benicio Moran (8)	28

Bedstone College, Bedstone

Ivy Armitage-Pryce (9)	29
Sophia Smith-Hughes (10)	30
Lucy Dahn (9)	31
Grace Woodhead (10)	32
Cecily Halford (11)	33

Doddinghurst Church Of England Junior School, Doddinghurst

Evie Etherington (9)	34
Chloe Boyle (9) & Esme Holland (9)	35
Emily Jones (10) & Lois Singh (10)	36
Ivy Holland (10)	37
Harlan Harris (9) & Michael Capps (9)	38
Alfie Hardy (10) & Frankie	39
Ralph Nicholls (9) & Zac Niyazi (9)	40
Alex Davies (9)	41
Josh Endean-Dalby (10) & Riley Clough (10)	42
Enya Hesse (9)	43
Sophie Barton (9)	44

Downsview Primary School, Swanley

Felix Donnellan (10)	45
Henry Hall (9)	46
Kayden Cook (10)	47
Lois Butler (10)	48
Jax Colasanto (9)	49
Jessica E (9)	50
Asten Fairweather (10)	51
Amelia McAleese	52

Jessica W (9)	53
Kacie Buckley (9)	54
Reagan Spearman-Millins (10)	55
Calum Harding (9)	56
Bobby Belmont (10)	57
Ellie-May Napper (9)	58
Nathan Lee (10)	59
Nicolas Sitarski (9)	60
Henry Wells (9)	61
Isabella Champion (10)	62

Forge Wood Primary School, Crawley

Marcel Bogatkiewicz (11)	63
Nayonika Sujitkumar (11)	64
Varshika Reddy Dodda (11)	65
Aahil Muhammad Arafat (11)	66
Jamie Russell (11)	67

Kinson Academy, Kinson

Maisie Whiffen (8)	68
Faith March (7)	69
Isabella Akanbi (7)	70
Liberty Hyde (8)	71

Loddiswell Primary School, Loddiswell

Callum Weeks (10)	72
Emily Woodward (10)	73
Liberty Motson (10)	74
Archie Ball (11)	75
Theo Cater (10)	76

Metheringham Primary School, Metheringham

Harry Vickers (7)	77
Thomas Creasey (9)	78
Annabelle Washington (9)	79
Hugh Herring (8)	80
Cleo Newell (7)	81
Roseanne Saffin (8)	82

Monymusk School, Monymusk

Emma Donaldson (9)	83
Nathan Houston (10)	84
Lewis Gourley (9)	85
Erin Wood (9)	86
Aubrey Miceal (8)	87
Josh Musselwhite (8)	88
Jude McKenzie (9)	89
Jacob Field (9)	90

Ryedene Primary & Nursery School, Vange

Halle Pardoe (9)	91
Abigail Ncube (9)	92
Evie Knight (10)	93
Tommy Smith (10)	94
Munachi Udorji (10)	95
Archie Victory (9)	96
Hollie Che (10)	97
Taylor-Grace Stare (9)	98
Logan Painter (9)	99
Layla Hyde (10)	100
Millie Pope (9)	101
Timmy Ganiyu (10)	102
Jayden Roberts (10)	103
Scarlett Pearce (10)	104
Bella Roberts (10)	105
Layla Guzel (9)	106
Brodie Loveday (10)	107
Marshall Dell-Murphy (10)	108
Reagan Williams Cooper (10)	109
Meadow Dowson (9)	110

Shawhead Primary School, Shawhead

Sophie Truesdale (10)	111
Katie Cockburn (12)	112
Sophie-Mae Johnstone (10)	113
Angela Slavin (10)	114
Sammie Sharp (11)	115

St Clare's Catholic Primary School, Handsworth

Rida Fatima (11)	116
Fedora Nkrumah (10)	117
Seim Teklesenbet (10)	118
Goodness Nlemoha (10)	119
Nazakat Hussain (10)	120
Alayna-Jannah Adam (11)	121
Ameera Hussain (9)	122
Joan Chinedu (11)	123
Jessica Chinedu (10)	124
Ameera Jannat Ali (10)	125
Joan Chinedu (11)	126

St John's Catholic Junior School, Bebington

Ella Haggerty (10)	127
Sophia Reynolds (10)	128
Evie Pettersson (9)	129

St Mary's Catholic Primary School, Bognor Regis

Ray Johnson (11)	130
Benjamin Dlugaszek (10)	131
Izzy Skeef (11)	132
Lucas Law (10)	133
Lexi Hickey (7)	134
Jan Spiewak (9)	135
Florence Burles (9)	136
Merson Cooper (10)	137

Thistle Hill Academy, Minster-On-Sea

Heidi Rumbold (10)	138
Kai Llufrio (9)	139
Ava-Sophia Monks (10)	140

Walpole Highway Primary School, Wisbech

Viktoria Limontaite (9)	141
Charlie Saward (9)	142
Ciara Shinn (10)	143
Holly Hill (10)	144
Emi Webb (10)	145
Harry Saward (7)	146
Araminta Chamberlain (9)	147
Logan Lord (7)	148
Albie Sadrija (9)	149
Mason Nicholls (9)	150
Vinnie Webster (9)	151
Bailey Hogg (8)	152
Billie Panks (8)	153
Flynn Roberts (9)	154
Taylor Hogg (8)	155

THE STORIES

Monster Slayer

Dragging through the thick, everlasting snow, Kora trudged on. Trying to find something. "At last!" Kora exclaimed, stepping into the centre of five towering pillars. Scavenging through his backpack, he held up a glistening gem and began to chant. "Gem of sacrifice, summoner of darkness, arise, master of sanguine blood art!" Beams pointed directly at the crystal. Kora drew his sword. Suddenly, a ferocious fight took place. The determined fighter knew what he had to do. "With this treasure, I summon! Destroyer of dimensions, crafter of power... Maharaja!" Out of nowhere, a sacred sword slashed the blood arts master in half.

Tawana Sithole (10)
Ardeley St Lawrence CE (VA) Primary School, Ardeley

Daydreamer

Gentle Lady Heart was daydreaming about swimming five hundred metres when suddenly, she got whisked away to Planet Malow (that always happened when someone was getting sad). Lady Heart got out her wand and looked for someone she needed to help. In the distance, she could hear some loud, big tears, so she rushed over to find an upset alien called Slime-Bob! Clever Lady Heart used her magical powers to suck out all the worries and troubles in his head, which indeed was very slimy!

Instantly, he felt much happier and joyful! "Thank you!" said Slime-Bob gratefully. Her work was done, and she was back, daydreaming again!

Annabelle York (7)

Ardeley St Lawrence CE (VA) Primary School, Ardeley

Autumn's Terrific Life

One lovely, sun-blinding day, Autumn's mum gave birth to her. Unexpectedly, Ohio was born straight after Autumn, which meant they were... twins!
One day, Autumn went out with Ohio. "Autumn, I don't think this is safe. We don't know how to swim and we can't breathe underwater. It's not like we're mermaids, we might drown," said Ohio.
"Don't be silly, it's fine. I know how to from watching Mum and Dad. I know how to so I can teach you if you want?" answered Autumn.
"Are you sure you know how to, Autumn?"
They dived into the ocean...

Annabelle Krieger (10)
Ardeley St Lawrence CE (VA) Primary School, Ardeley

Fiery Friendship

One fine day, a dragon stickman lived in a faraway country. He decided to fly to a tiny village to see his friends. Having fun, he jumped for joy and accidentally set the jail alight. The prisoners escaped. The police came and rounded all the mean prisoners up, and the firemen put out the fire. The villagers asked Mighty Maroon, the stickman dragon, to leave the village and live in the mountains so he didn't accidentally set anything else on fire. The dragon happily started making himself at home in a cave on a mountain.

Toby Ballard (8)

Ardeley St Lawrence CE (VA) Primary School, Ardeley

Glidy And His Journey To Find A Friend

One day, there was a boy named Glidy. He was on a journey to find friendship because he wanted a friend. He set out to find a friend.

He found a dog, but he was scared of him. After a few minutes, he thought he should be friends with other monsters, so he went to Monster Village. When he got there, he went to the park. There were loads of other monsters and kids. Then he asked a girl who was all alone to be his friend. She said, "Yes. I am in need of a friend, too."

Grace Koop (8)

Ardeley St Lawrence CE (VA) Primary School, Ardeley

The Big Bang!

96,000 years ago scientists discovered a green, pink, blue, purple and black egg. The egg was found in 2014, Monday 8th April on a beach in Cornwall, England.

Eight years later, there was a big explosion and the egg cracked... Seconds later it hatched a cute baby Exvackulaaj monster.

A few years later... it was bigger than any mythical creature. It found a scientist and they became friends. After that, it tracked back to Nalabadedjax...

Hudson Streatfield (9)

Ardeley St Lawrence CE (VA) Primary School, Ardeley

Fluffy's Adventure

Far away, there lived a monster called Fluffy. He was on a walk when he fell through the clouds and landed on Earth.

"Where am I?" Fluffy said to himself. He saw a dog, "Argh! I need to run away!" he said, scared.

He hid behind a house; he was safe then. He flew home, but he hit his head! A bird pushed him home though! And then he was in bed.

Rogue Baker (8)
Ardeley St Lawrence CE (VA) Primary School, Ardeley

Snow Disaster

One day, a little girl came outside to make a snowman. She called it Snowman Monster. The Snowman Monster came to life. The little girl ran home and the Snowman Monster made lots more snowmen, and they said, "Let's go to Iceland!" They made friends and had fun, and the little girl never came back.

Chloe Wilkinson (9)
Ardeley St Lawrence CE (VA) Primary School, Ardeley

Jackabong

Once upon a time, there was a gruesome monster who threw himself off Mars and landed on Earth. A person called James caught him.

The monster's name was Jackabong and it said, "Can you be my friend?"

"Of course I can. Can you drive?" asked James.

"No, I can't."

"Good thing you have me. Should we go to McDonald's?" asked James.

"I'll try it."

"Okay, let's go. Is it okay if you wait for half an hour?"

"Okay."

"We're here. Wait, what do you want?"

"Mars chocolate cake."

"Okay, Mars chocolate cake. Let's drive forward... Okay, let's eat."

Adam Maniyar (8)
Avon House Preparatory School, Woodford Green

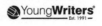

You Are Cool

100,000 years ago, there were monsters everywhere on Mars. One time, there was a person called Dhilan. He said, "Hello."
The aliens said, "Beblo."
And that was confusing, wasn't it? Dhilan thought he was in a new world. He did not know what they were saying. He was thinking something. He said, "Goodbye."
Then the aliens said, "Food ny!"
Dhilah said, "Oh, bother."
The aliens said, "So sother."
He went to get his hammer. He banged each alien. The bigger they got, the kinder they got, and nicer, they got cooler.
"You are cooler than before," said Dhilan.

Dhilan Mistry (7)
Avon House Preparatory School, Woodford Green

The Monster

Once, in Candyland there was brave and heroic Aliyaan. He set off for a space mission. As he zoomed his spacecraft, it hit an asteroid and landed on Planet Bogland. There he saw an enormous monster. Aliyaan was baffled and astonished. For a second he thought it was a dream so kept rubbing his eyes vigorously but the monster was still there. Blood trickled down from its mouth as it roared loudly. "I want to have a feast, yum-yum!"
He briskly grabbed and attacked Aliyaan! Aliyaan acted hypersonic and sprinted away from the protruding eyes of the monster. He hopped in his aircraft and dashed away... *Whoosh!*

Muhammad Aliyaah Atif (8)
Avon House Preparatory School, Woodford Green

11

Mission Scary

It was night-time. Mr Crazy Nine Eyes was sleeping. Suddenly, an alarm sounded!
He leapt out of bed and slid down the pole.
Captain Crazypants was saying, "You need to rescue Alien Dory urgently!" so off he went.
He used his jetpack to get there quickly and landed on Planet Spike. He heard Dory shouting, "Help! I'm lost!"
Nine Eyes leapt across a fiery chasm and grabbed her tightly. They zoomed back to headquarters.
Mr Crazy Nine Eyes darted his eyes around excitedly while he was showered with gold, silver, emeralds, rubies and sapphires as a reward for rescuing Dory.

Azrael Gale (8)
Avon House Preparatory School, Woodford Green

Viper And The Defeat

A hundred years ago, a child called Theo had trouble with a monster called Viper. Viper would destroy a house every year. Sadly, Theo's friend's house was broken. Each year, Viper was getting closer than ever before to Theo's house...
Forty years later, Theo's house was destroyed. He had to fight back. As he tiptoed, he heard a voice: "Fighters all ready." Viper dashed out of the darkness! Theo plunged the sword into the beast's body. The beast slammed to the ground. Theo had won! Robin, Theo's dad, was so happy. The king made Theo king for a hundred years.

Theo Duncan (7)
Avon House Preparatory School, Woodford Green

13

The Fox, The Boy And The B.E.A.R.

Once there was an alien fox called Butterfly and her enemy was called B.E.A.R. One day Pluto, her planet, was going to explode. Just before, her mother said to her, "Be brave on Earth and stay out of sight." Mother put Butterfly into the pod. Twenty years later Butterfly decided to visit the town and as she went through the gate she met a boy. She said, "Will you help me defeat B.E.A.R.?" The boy said, "Yes."

They went to B.E.A.R. and fought him. They soon won. They took B.E.A.R.'s arm and buried it in the soil. They became friends.

Alanna Sarker-Islam (8)
Avon House Preparatory School, Woodford Green

Brutal Luinor Strikes Back

One day, Brutal Luinor was fighting Belfyre, but then Belfyre quit. After Belfyre quit the stage, Luinor heard a crash! He saw a mermaid. Luinor gave a roar, then the scared mermaid ran away and bumped into Fanfair. The mermaid said, "I put up a big fight."

"Okay, okay," said Fanfair. "I will get my gun because I will kill him myself."

So he went to Luinor. Luinor said, "Why are you here?"

Fanfair said, "I've come to kill you."

So Luinor bit him in the neck and pulled it off so Fanfair would die completely.

Yusuf Zayaan (7)
Avon House Preparatory School, Woodford Green

Once Upon A Time In Germany

Once upon a time on Earth, a kind monster was born. She grew up to be truthful, kind and clever. One day, she went for a picnic. She saw the perfect forest to eat her picnic. She saw a girl called Ruby. They saw each other and walked over and introduced themselves and became friends. They had the picnic. They realised they were lost. Then the girl got her projector and did the SOS sign. Someone realised and came and took them home. They said, "Never, never, never go to the forest on your own." They went back to their own homes.

Yorkshire Swarbrick (8)
Avon House Preparatory School, Woodford Green

Tom On Uranus

Once upon a time, there was a friendly monster called Leo. On Uranus, Leo woke up to see uranium rain noisily pattering on his window. Then a silver spaceship landed. The captain was called Tom the captain. Tom hadn't eaten, so his lunch was in his carriage. Tom went into Leo's house. Tom wanted to share his lunch, but he didn't know what Leo ate, so he gave him rice. Leo seemed to like it. When Tom finished, he decided that he would go, but Leo insisted that he stay. Leo and his friends built a house out of uranium bricks.

Ethan Cai (7)
Avon House Preparatory School, Woodford Green

Once Upon A Time On Earth

Once upon a time, there lived a crazy, evil monster who attacked people in the future. One day, magically it was transported to the present. It was very unsure and still attacked people there. There were lots of people and they were all in hiding spots that couldn't be found. Nearly everyone was eaten. The monster's name was Hagger. One day, there was a brave warrior who was a girl. Her name was Pearl. When Pearl went up to Hagger, a dangerous fight began. Then, a portal opened and Pearl pushed Hagger into it. He was defeated.

Amaya Randerwala (7)
Avon House Preparatory School, Woodford Green

Devil Of Doom And Bright Brave The Brave

Once upon a time, there was a monster called Devil of All Doom. Devil of All Doom lived in the enchanted cave. In those times, there were no monsters, but he was the most feared across the land!
Not far, there was the Land of Knight. One day, Devil attacked. That made Brave the Brave angry, so he decided to kill him. Soon, he was ready to set off. Soon, he reached the place. He saw the monster crying. The monster looked up and saw Brave and felt scared. Suddenly, he stabbed Devil and everyone cheered for Brave.

Aarit Gandhi (7)
Avon House Preparatory School, Woodford Green

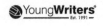

Lola And Emorkus

Once upon a time, there was this girl. She had everything except for one thing... a friend. Her name was Lola. She had tried making a friend, but it never worked in her whole entire life. She was very sad about it.

When she was fourteen, this monster came to her house. The monster was named Emorkus. He was extremely fat. He had seen the little girl be upset. He rang the doorbell. She wasn't scared. She actually loved the monster! The monster had special powers that could turn sad people into happy people.

Xyla Bygrave (8)

Avon House Preparatory School, Woodford Green

Vegeta Vs Goku

Vegeta and Goku were enemies. They met in a shop and Vegeta said, "Do you want to fight?" Goku said, "Yes. After I have bought my food, meet me in the battle arena!"

"Okay."

So Goku flew back to his home and said to his wife, "I need to eat a ton of food."

She said, "Yes," so Goku ate rice, cookies, apples, bananas, pears, chocolate, and many more foods. Goku went to the arena and saw Vegeta and Goku did a Kamehameha and beat Vegeta - just!

Kaelan Kaelas (8)
Avon House Preparatory School, Woodford Green

21

A Journey To Earth

One day, Fuzzy was bored, so he decided to look for something to do. Suddenly, he came across a big skyscraping cube. As he was very curious, he touched it and, *zap!* He disappeared!

All of a sudden, he found himself in a field of green. Where was he? He saw a man approach him. He told Fuzzy that he was called James and that he would help Fuzzy get home. So he took him to a gigantic building. It was a space station. Cheekily, Fuzzy stole a spaceship and off they went, back to the Planet of Fuzz.

Max Springett (8)

Avon House Preparatory School, Woodford Green

Monsters At Livan

Many years ago, there was the city of Livan. Only monsters could live there. A monster called Vantenshedi was the King of Livan. He was in a conflict with the Viking Monsters.

In time, an accident happened and the king said, "What is the accident?"

One hundred cars had crashed at the same time. Then another accident happened and the king saw that three cars had dropped into the sea. But everything was good and, by the end, the king got tired and fell asleep. No one could wake him up.

Jacob Srokowski (7)

Avon House Preparatory School, Woodford Green

Yusuf Shrunk Rock Rack

Once there was a scientist called Yusuf who made a robot called Rock Rack and a machine called Shrinker. When he finished making Rock Rack he wanted to shrink him. So he got it to shrink him and Booya. He shrunk and Rock Rack was scared, Yusuf looked around on the floor but could not find him. Rock Rack was lost but he was found, or was he?
A few hours later Rock Rack was found on the ground in the laboratory. Yusuf made him normal again like he was before and they ate their super supper.

Yusuf Ishfaq (8)

Avon House Preparatory School, Woodford Green

Stitch The Great

Once upon a time, Stitch was the kindest monster in the world. He lived in a mansion made of hot dogs.

A girl named Salqua came and took Stitch! *Dun, dun, dun, dun!* You get the hang of this. Right, back to the story... He was put in a toy shop.

At night it was dark. A girl bought him. He was very angry he'd been taken.

He thought this was the end, but it was not. He escaped and went back to his hot dog mansion.

Aiden Bhandari (7)
Avon House Preparatory School, Woodford Green

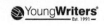

The Monster And The Girl

A long time ago, Kreem was in Wales and he did not have any friends. He was very sad. Then he saw a girl he wanted to play with but she was sad because her mum was very ill. Kreem was sad for her and had an idea to cheer her up. He went to play with her and she was happy and they have been friends ever since. She had a dog called Stitch, he was a very good dog then she had two chameleons and a cat and fish. He also had a chameleon.

Nia Biston (8)

Avon House Preparatory School, Woodford Green

The Poo Poo Monster

Once upon a time, there was a scientist, a lonely one. He had two children who died of sickness so he turned himself into a monster. Yes, a monster! The monster was called Shaneequa. The monster/Shaneequa lost his memory when he turned into a monster.

One day he saw a girl and he fell in love. She ran for her life and did a gigantic fart and the fart turned him back into the scientist. He lived to bully ever after.

Ezra B

Avon House Preparatory School, Woodford Green

27

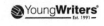

The Death Battle

One day, two evil monsters awoke in the sea. Up above on land, children were playing football at the Olympics. Suddenly, both monsters jumped on land and started fighting. Death Eater punched Igoigo into the Science Museum, so Igoigo kicked the Death Eater into Hyde Park, so the Death Eater threw his trident and electrocuted Igoigo and hung Igoigo on the Eiffel Tower.

Benicio Moran (8)

Avon House Preparatory School, Woodford Green

Bouncy's Adventure

Once upon a time, in Bouncy Land, Bouncy is sent away to Jolly Land after he argues with his friend, Bob. Bouncy is scared, frightened and alone. He stumbles across his arch-enemy, Jolly. Bouncy runs into a dark, lonely cave. Seeing light through the cave he adventures further through to find the light but it is a party for the Jollingtons. Bouncy tries to find his way back, then he realises it is a trap! *Crash*! The walls become a prison. Through a crack in the wall, two eyes appear, Jolly! Astonishingly, Jolly saves Bouncy from the cave. Yay!

Ivy Armitage-Pryce (9)
Bedstone College, Bedstone

29

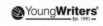

Wobble Monster

One day, Wobble Monster decided he would be scary because he had never been scary before. After that day, Wobble went into his pipes and slithered around the floor in a local nursery until he found a cute little girl's water bottle, which he hid in until lunchtime. While she was eating her lunch, Wobble unscrewed the water bottle and decided he would rock the bottle and spill himself everywhere and scare all the children. When he poured himself on the table, he chickened out and ended up apologising to the little girl.

Sophia Smith-Hughes (10)
Bedstone College, Bedstone

Barry

There is a monster called Barry; he is a slimy, wet blob. He likes to scare people by bouncing up and down on the floor, and he is so enormous because he eats all the food in your house. One day, he ate too much food, and then suddenly, exploded into small, tiny Barrys, and they ate all the food in the house within two seconds. All the Barrys kept going to random places and eating their food so whenever you see a slimy wet blob that will be Barry so watch out, he might eat all your food.

Lucy Dahn (9)
Bedstone College, Bedstone

31

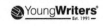

The Bestie Monster

Katie is my best friend but she is also a goat in disguise, she claims to be human but last week, when I lost my homework, my excuse was my best friend ate it because I caught Katie on the sofa eating it.

Three days later I caught her trying to eat my maths homework but this time by the river with a side of grass. She's a little crazy but she has ten times won the homework-eating sports in the Olympics. So if you ever wonder why you lost your homework then look at Katie.

Grace Woodhead (10)

Bedstone College, Bedstone

Crusty Musty Red Crab And The Mayonnaise

Once upon a time, there lived a red crab called Crusty Musty Red Crab. His fear was mayonnaise. One day, Crusty Musty Red Crab went on holiday to the beach, but he did not see what was coming. Crusty Musty Red Crab found a nice cave to stay in for a couple of nights.

Then in the morning, one girl had fish and chips for her lunch. She had mayonnaise on it.

The little girl saw Crusty Musty Red Crab and went into his cave. The red crab pushed the fish and chips.

Cecily Halford (11)
Bedstone College, Bedstone

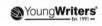

The Fantastic Fuzzys

There lived three Fuzzys: Fuzzy, Buzzy and Jazzy. They live in a world full of candy. Although candy's unhealthy in our world, it's healthy in their world. In fact, the only thing they eat is candy, candy and candy! So let's get to know the Fuzzys. Fuzzy loves football, Buzzy loves puzzles, and Jazzy loves jazz (it's probably obvious from his name, but in their language they would say 'glob glob glob'. But Buzzy speaks English, not Fuzzyain. Now, unfortunately, the Fuzzys have to go. See you in the next one!
"Bye!"
"Glob!"
"Glob!"
"Glob!"

Evie Etherington (9)
Doddinghurst Church Of England Junior School, Doddinghurst

The Story Of Beavile's Lifetime!

Unfortunately, Beavile's mum and dad split up. For some reason, the dad wanted to be evil, so he took Neavile and became evil. Then, Beavile's mum, Mumvile, wanted Beavile to go to school. The next day Mumvile signed Beavile up for school, six hours later Mumvile got a text message which said: 'Dear Mumvile, I have to inform you that Beavile is gladly allowed to come to Beavile Town School!'
Excited to tell Beavile she skipped along to Beavile's bedroom. Once she told Beavile the next next day she dropped off Beavile at his new school that he would love!

Chloe Boyle (9) & Esme Holland (9)

Doddinghurst Church Of England Junior School, Doddinghurst

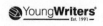

Oscar's Crazy Adventure Finding His Lost Brother

One day in Crazy Wonderland, Oscar suddenly noticed his brother was missing, so he set off on an adventure. He said goodbye to his village and came across footprints of his brother. They led to a house full of humans. They took him to a cave with a lock. Oscar heard a scream saying, "It's me, Colin!"

Oscar asked to let him out. The humans gave Oscar the key.

Oscar and Colin returned to their home and they greeted Colin and threw him a party.

Unexpectedly, they found a secret door that had a fantastic room full of excitement and books.

Emily Jones (10) & Lois Singh (10)

Doddinghurst Church Of England Junior School, Doddinghurst

Slime War

It was an ordinary, slimetastic day in Slime Land until Greeny Groo started to get on Slime Susan's nerves. Slimy Susan kept on telling him to stop, but he did not stop. So a humongous war broke out into a slime war. *Sploosh! Crash! Bang!* Slimy Susan, with her marvellous pink goop, sprayed Greeny Groo, so he picked up his green gloop and... *Whoosh!* Slimy Susan fell to the ground. Greeny Groo ran over to Slimy Susan, she got up. *Boom!* Greeny Groo held his ground but a magic potion spilt suddenly. They turned into humans.

Ivy Holland (10)
Doddinghurst Church Of England Junior School, Doddinghurst

Moosy Mobs

There once was an alien called Moofoxdo. Moofoxdo had a lot of enemies, including Earthlings and Martians. He lived on a dwarf planet called Pluto. On Pluto, the Martians were dying, so he came down to Earth. That was where the Martian's super fortress was located. The battle commenced on 14th of June, 2090 at 6am in the morning. The Martians fought for their lives, trying to defeat Moofoxdo, but he was too strong so he wiped them all out.

After the battle, the losses were unbearable. Families mourned in despair for their loved ones.

Harlan Harris (9) & Michael Capps (9)

Doddinghurst Church Of England Junior School, Doddinghurst

Spocoboggle Vs Feeble The Third

Feeble ate Spocoboggle's door and said, "I challenge you to a battle?" So they fought and it was an extremely close fight, and Feeble was very close to winning, but Spocoboggle never ever gave up. After that, it was a 50/50 chance of winning and neither of them gave up. They both summoned a very, very, very powerful sword, which led to both of them being badly injured, but that didn't stop them. Spocoboggle got Feeble on the floor and finished him off for the next 300 years!

Alfie Hardy (10) & Frankie
Doddinghurst Church Of England Junior School, Doddinghurst

Fortnite SnakeHead And Peter Griffin

Firstly, SnakeHead is from the Matrix and he went into a teleport and went into Fortnite chapter five, season two map. So he went to Spawn Island and hopped onto the battle bus. Snake Head jumped off the battle bus, then went to Snooty Steps aka Peter Griffin's place. He got out his glider and landed directly at Peter Griffin's lair. Now he can get Peter's medallion and the vault to win the game and get around W. When he got them he killed the whole lobby in thirty seconds.

Ralph Nicholls (9) & Zac Niyazi (9)
Doddinghurst Church Of England Junior School, Doddinghurst

Sevan's Takeover

Once upon a time, there lived a vicious snake called Sevan. He lived on a planet called Plant Vismon. Sevan was a lonely monster, so one day, he thought of taking over the world! So, on a mysterious flipchart, he started to plan.
Once he was ready, he started. He took one monster down at a time. When he took the monsters down, he went to Earth. When he got there, he took every human down...

Alex Davies (9)

Doddinghurst Church Of England Junior School, Doddinghurst

Pikachu Becomes A Hero

Pikachu met a friend called Ash. He went to a coffee shop and found Ash. He put him into a Poké Ball and he lived there until Ash found someone to fight. Pikachu came out of the Poké Ball and fought his worst enemy. He shot lightning out of his hands and made his enemy back away but he came back and attacked Pikachu again. Pikachu shot tunnels at him and he defeated him.

Josh Endean-Dalby (10) & Riley Clough (10)

Doddinghurst Church Of England Junior School, Doddinghurst

The Fight

Swambly was sitting in the sewers and then he started to swim deeper and deeper into the sewers. There, he found his arch-enemy planning to blow up the city! Swambly had the energy to have a fight in the sewers, so they started to fight. *Boom! Bang! Pow! Crash!* But then they were out of breath, so they both stopped fighting and both ran away.

Enya Hesse (9)
Doddinghurst Church Of England Junior School, Doddinghurst

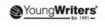

The Food Fight In The Café

It was a boiling afternoon and Phoebe the crazy monster was practising gymnastics in the school café. This made her extremely sweaty. However, she was having a spectacular time, until she spotted Horrible Hannah, her worst enemy ever! Suddenly, they started fighting, throwing food at each other and laughing at each other.

Sophie Barton (9)
Doddinghurst Church Of England Junior School, Doddinghurst

The Sun's Batteries

"The sun has turned off and we need someone to turn it back on," called out the Prime Minister of Zlorb.

"I will!" shouted Octo-Wobble.

So he squeezed his spacesuit over his hat and put on his jetpack. And off he flew with batteries in his hands.

When he reached the sun, Octo-Wobble was boiling. He searched for the battery compartment for hours on end, and when he finally found it, Octo-Wobble replaced the batteries.

After he had flown back to Zlorb, there were many celebrations.

"Octo-Wobble, Octo-Wobble, Octo-Wobble!" the aliens chanted.

"Ahhhhhh..." he sighed in much joy.

Felix Donnellan (10)
Downsview Primary School, Swanley

45

How A Monster Saves Humanity

Octa Blob, the slimy, dark blue creature, teleported through the night sky on a mission to find his crazy, cracked-up duplicate, looking to destroy the world. Octa starts his mission by gathering resources to take his duplicate Octa Bib out. Octa has made a sword and teleports to Octa Bib's haunted, abandoned castle. Octa is ready to be a hero. He stabs the door, but his sword shatters into pieces.

"No!" he declares in loss. He doesn't give up, and he goes in with bare hands. He spots Octo and attacks one more hit.

"Yes!" Octa Blob screams. Octa Bib was defeated.

Henry Hall (9)
Downsview Primary School, Swanley

46

Crazy Monster Planet

One day, a crazy monster named Bob flew to Crazy Monster Planet, and Bob's enemy flew to Bob's planet. He looked like a giant, naughty cyclops-yeti and Bob looked like a clever, horned, four-eyed monster.

Bob and his enemy started a giant fight. Bob used his lasers to shoot at his enemy. His enemy's powers were he could fly and Ground Punch.

Bob made his enemy fly away in his rocket. Bob was the giant fright. Bob made himself a superhero.

Bob's enemy flew back to Crazy Creature Planet and took Bob down again. Bob was crying and pleading.

Kayden Cook (10)
Downsview Primary School, Swanley

The Bestest Fighting Friends

One day, a boy called Gloogle had an enemy called Ooglebooglooogle. He *hated* Gloogle. They didn't know if they wanted to fight or not. They were both really scared, but one day, they decided to fight. Ooglebooglooogle fought Gloogle and Ooglebooglooogle fell over. Gloogle wasn't mean, so he helped him up. They started to talk to each other and very, very, very slowly became really good friends. They hung out every day for ten minutes. They had lots of fun, so they hung out every day for two hours. They got along very, very well. I hope they are okay.

Lois Butler (10)

Downsview Primary School, Swanley

The Naughty Toblablob And The Kids

One night, two kids were exploring the creepy, dark forest, but they saw a big, deep, long cave. They went in and saw an orange creature. It only stared, but then they saw it move. It was going to a door. *Whoosh!* They were all sucked in. It was pretty, but scary. They then saw a spitting image of the monster they'd just found.
He screeched, "War!"
The children ran for cover and watched the monster fight his... brother! They were both lunging at each other. Suddenly, Toblablob defeated it with a push. The kids went home after that.

Jax Colasanto (9)
Downsview Primary School, Swanley

Fred's Survival For WWII

One day Fred went on an adventure to find food, but he didn't know that the country was going to war that day. Then he heard sirens but didn't know what the sirens were for. He was worried and tried to get as much food as he could. He wasn't thinking and killed an animal, the animal was a caterpillar.

Fred said, "Oh no!" but Fred didn't like other animals so Fred carried on like nothing had happened. He rushed to his hideout to hide out so he didn't get bombed. He saw people getting evacuated. Would he ever see them again?

Jessica E (9)
Downsview Primary School, Swanley

Ooga Booga And The Haunted House

There once was a monster called Ooga Booga and he was exploring a haunted house. He went into one room, it was the dingy and dusty bathroom. He went into the dusty, crusty bedroom. At the corner of his eye, he saw the bed covers move. He moved the covers and there was Schreech, his enemy. Schreech jumped out of bed. Schreech took one punch, and Ooga Booga took the other. Ooga Booga shot snot out of his nose. Schreech dodged the snot until they realised that they shouldn't fight and should be friends. They shook hands and they are now friends.

Asten Fairweather (10)
Downsview Primary School, Swanley

51

Lurking, Looming Lemin The Lemon!

It all began in a seemingly normal grocery store. The victim, Posy, was walking down the fruit and vegetable aisle. She was buying ingredients for a lemon soup. She bought a pack of lemons, which included Lemin, who ate furniture when he was angry. Uh-oh! Posy was soon to have no furniture. Later that day, Posy made her marvellously famous lemon soup. When she was picking out her lemons, she didn't pick Lemin the angry lemon. He was so angry that he ate all of the remaining furniture in the land!
The ghastly lemon strikes again!

Amelia McAleese
Downsview Primary School, Swanley

Goga Vs Bailey

One morning, in outer space, Goga and Bailey, who are both monsters, were playing on the moon. Then Goga was going to jump off the moon. Bailey wanted to jump off the moon first, but so did Goga. So they started to fight each other. They were fully punching each other, and then Goga fell on the moon, so Goga got up and pushed Bailey to the floor. Then Bailey got up, and they started to fight and fight and fight until they both finally stopped and said, "Why don't we both jump off at the same time? Three, two, one, go! Weeee!"

Jessica W (9)
Downsview Primary School, Swanley

53

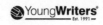

The Race To Space

One day, an alien from Bloogel Land, called Bloogel, went to Earth to explore, but people feared him. But, not just of him, a big creature was behind him. It was his arch-enemy, Joyful Jimmy. He said, "Blah, urgh, da," which meant 'race to space', so that's what they did.
Bloogel tried to leave Jimmy in his slime, but he was catching up. Bloogel was so close back to home, and Jimmy was too. Bloogel thought he would win, and he thought he had won the race to space, but Jimmy was not happy.

Kacie Buckley (9)

Downsview Primary School, Swanley

Rex And The Four Emeralds

One day, a T-rex called Rex accidentally broke his UFO and the only way to fix it was by getting emeralds. Firstly, he went to Earth and found the emerald, so he grabbed it, fought off a demon and escaped. Then, he went to his world and fought rhinos and stole their emeralds. Then, he went to Water Land, put a mask on and fought hammerhead sharks, getting their emerald. Finally, he went to Robot Land. But before he grabbed it, he fought a giant robot and escaped it. He placed the emeralds in and said, "Mission complete!"

Reagan Spearman-Millins (10)

Downsview Primary School, Swanley

55

The Zapper And The Meaty Badger

One day there was a battle over who would be the ruler of Mars. Luckily the actual king won. So everyone was safe. But one day The Meaty Badger came along. He made everyone his slave after he beat the king. But a year later The Zapper came along and challenged The Meaty Badger. The Meaty Badger was getting lots of hits on The Zapper. The Zapper was hitting The Meaty Badger with his tail and zapping him. The Zapper won the battle and set everyone free and also gave everyone free money.
"You all get £100 each."

Calum Harding (9)
Downsview Primary School, Swanley

The Crazy Slimeball

One day, Bobbel woke up and heard Slime Ball's splash on Crazy Creature Planet. Bobbel went outside and saw the evil Bobbel Planet destroy Crazy Creature Planet. It was sucking the Crazy Creature planet onto Evil Bobbel Planet. Then Evil Bobbel was trying to find Bobbel. Bobbel saw Evil Bobbel. Bobbel used his Bobbel hit, but Evil Bobbel hit his Evil Bobbel blast. Luckily, Bobbel dodged it and hit Evil Bobbel with his Bobbel explosion and shot Evil Bobbel off Crazy Creature Land and now he is named Bobbel the hero.

Bobby Belmont (10)
Downsview Primary School, Swanley

Candy Land

Buttercup and Lady were playing outside but a goblin came out of the shadows and attacked them.

"Oh no!" said Lady.

Buttercup and Lady fought them off.

"The goblin king is back," said Buttercup.

"Let's fly there," said Lady.

They flew there to defeat the goblin king. They ran in and killed the goblins and went to the goblin king. Buttercup and Lady finished him off. They flew back to Buttercup's castle and all the people were thanking them for saving them. Then they went to bed.

Ellie-May Napper (9)

Downsview Primary School, Swanley

The Story Of A Squid-Shark

One day, there was a shark, but it was no ordinary shark because it was part shark, part squid, and it could turn into a great white squid. The story begins when the squid shark is having fun in the water and sees a boy looking at him. The squid-shark was frightened at first, but after a bit, they became best friends. They played for a while before the boy's mother saw the squid-shark and petted the squid-shark, and then the squid-shark gave the boy to his mother. After he did, the squid-shark swam away.

Nathan Lee (10)
Downsview Primary School, Swanley

Plastic Problem

The Soap was going to Earth. He saw some plastic on the ground. The Soap was mad. He picked it up. "Why is this on the ground?" Then he put it in the bin. He was going on an adventure to find some plastic and put it in the bin. He was happy that he was doing this. He kept on doing it, on and on and on and on. When he finished he ran to his spaceship and said, "Goodbye." And he said, "See you later."

He put his engine on and flew away to a new planet.

Nicolas Sitarski (9)

Downsview Primary School, Swanley

Untitled

Once, there was a monster named Minotaur. He was really good at basketball, but no one believed him, so he wanted to prove them wrong. He went with his friends to the basketball court and skilled them all up. They were shocked to see him do it. They all said, "Wow!" in shock. They all said, "You can play in the monster league!"
He didn't know what that was, so his friends explained. He wanted to play but he was too young to play, but he still tried.

Henry Wells (9)
Downsview Primary School, Swanley

Crazy Bob And His Enemy

Crazy Bob's enemy, Crazy Jay, was arguing about something, but they didn't know who to pick, so they decided to fight, so they did. Bob left because he was in a spaceship, as was Crazy Jay. They were fighting in spaceships with lasers and slime shooting at each other, but their spaceships broke, so they used turbo blasters to fight, but they broke as well, so they had to fight by hand. Crazy Bob can fly, but Crazy Jay can't, so Crazy Bob won the fight.

Isabella Champion (10)
Downsview Primary School, Swanley

Tom And Penut

One day Tom spotted a creature lying on the floor not far from his house. He walked up to the creature and asked what he was called.

The creature replied, "Penut."

Tom politely asked, "Why are you here?"

Penut said, "I was visiting Earth from the Callifice planet. Tom, do you want to help me find my UFO?"

Tom said, "Let's go."

Tom and Penut headed off to find Penut's UFO. They went to Cornwall, no luck. Then Crawley, still no luck. After, they headed off to London where they eventually found Penut's UFO.

Penut said, "Thank you!"

Marcel Bogatkiewicz (11)

Forge Wood Primary School, Crawley

63

Candyland Chaos

One calm afternoon, Twinkle was munching on some sweets in Candyland Wood. Suddenly, she heard thunder up ahead. Uh-oh, that must mean Shine, her enemy, was causing some mischief. In despair, Twinkle watched as Shine turned all the sweet plants to ashes. She couldn't stand it anymore and began to hatch a plan. Twinkle discovered that dust from a special gemstone called a Skyheart, would set things right. There was no time to waste! Quickly, Twinkle flew to the top of Mount Sugar. Rushing back to the woods, Twinkle sprinkled the dust. The plants bloomed back. Candyland was saved!

Nayonika Sujitkumar (11)
Forge Wood Primary School, Crawley

Daisy And The Storm

It was a sunny day in Enchanted Wood. A unidragon called Daisy was so happy that she turned invisible.

Just as Daisy sat on the lush grass, a storm started. It caused so much chaos. Luckily, Daisy had some magic dust that could calm storms. She flew up to see Spark the witch, her enemy. Daisy flew as fast as she could and sprinkled the dust above the clouds.

Soon, the storm went away and all the damage that had been made vanished, as if the storm had never happened.

Daisy flew down and lay on the grass. What an exciting day!

Varshika Reddy Dodda (11)
Forge Wood Primary School, Crawley

The Rise Of The Devil

One night, a devil was screaming in the sadness. He remembered how the Uwu angels laughed at him because he had horns growing out of his smooth, round head. Later, he got kicked out of the angel colony. He was stranded in the quiet city of Tokyo. He had dreaded that day. With no hesitation, he flew to the colony, grabbed his flame trident and was about to throw it at the master angel, but remembered to always be nice and kind-hearted. Suddenly a gold, shimmering halo appeared on his head, at that moment he was an angel!

Aahil Muhammad Arafat (11)

Forge Wood Primary School, Crawley

Slurp-Zilla Flavours The Land Of Bland Land

Once upon a time, many years ago, there was a land called Bland Land. A place without flavour. Many stomachs rumbled with disappointment. But wait! That was no stomach rumbling, that was Slurp-Zilla! A legendary Japanese Noodle Monster who shot rays of soy sauce and sprinkled wasabi in his wake.

"We are saved!" said the citizens of Bland Land. Slurp-Zilla had brought them new flavours. They then changed the name of their land to Tasty Town.

Jamie Russell (11)
Forge Wood Primary School, Crawley

67

Gonzon The Friendly Creature

Bang! Crash! Wallop! Gonzon had landed on Mars. All the toxic gases spilt out carelessly along the hot surface. The long-armed creatures jumped out to guard their home. "Hey! Don't trespass!"
"Sorry!" As Gonzon hopped back on the ship to go home, he saw a green and blue planet, so Gonzon decided to fly to it. As he emerged closer, he saw a sign that said, *Splatburger.* He saw something that looked similar to himself, and as the sun set, Gonzon was sure to go to the planet again soon, and he flew away back home.

Maisie Whiffen (8)

Kinson Academy, Kinson

The Creature Called Laci

A creature called Laci lived in a village in Africa.
She didn't have a lot of money, but she was happy.
She loved singing and reading every day.
She would tell stories under the tree to the children
in the twilight. Nobody liked her except Mime.
Mime and Laci were best friends.
One day, the teacher said everybody should write a
story about a girl. At lunchtime, Laci had a
sandwich. At home time, Laci went to the park,
then went home.
One day, Laci was reading a book called 'Girls'
when she saw her teacher. She said hi and bye.

Faith March (7)

Kinson Academy, Kinson

69

The Fearless Monster

Far, far away there is a monster called Ferrya Pollsa. He only comes out in autumn and winter. He has friends called Littya Makla and Zubal Camilya. They always go to Monster Island together. Ferrya Pollsa, Littya Makla and Zubal Camilya meet someone called Leana Leon. She tells them that something is following him. So Leana Leon made friends with them. "We should go to Lizzy for help," cries Zubal Camilya so they all start walking to Lizzy's house. She is not there but Ferrya Pollsa does not give up... So they go on a mission.

Isabella Akanbi (7)
Kinson Academy, Kinson

The Tale Of Mysterious The Monster

Mysterious is a crazy creature. He has more than one of everything. He has wings and is a gymnast. He can backflip in and on a tightrope. One day, Mysterious's enemies come along. They follow him everywhere and they will not go. Suddenly, the police are lurking behind the enemies. Instantly, out of the utmost surprise, the police pounce on the enemies and bring them to justice. A few days after the struggle, the enemies are in prison and Mysterious is safe. But they have pickaxes and may escape. Though, they may also stay in prison.

Liberty Hyde (8)
Kinson Academy, Kinson

Wonkly's Great Expedition

One day a six-eyed creature called Wonkly told his brother he wanted to fly from his home, Jupiter, to Earth. His brother, Winkly, wanted to stop him because he was a bully. Wonkly spent ages making a rocket and eventually, it was ready.

Just before Wonkly took off from Jupiter he saw an alien. The alien was pointing to the rocket and shouting. Wonkly looked out of the window and saw Winkly putting a hole in it.

In the end, the alien was too strong for Winkly and defeated him.

Wonkly got to see Planet Earth after all.

Callum Weeks (10)

Loddiswell Primary School, Loddiswell

Leobro The Mingol And The Golden Sugar Fruit

In Buckiter Jungle, it was time for Leobro the Mingol to harvest the Golden Sugar Fruit, which gave all the Mingol Chicks their super strength. He travelled to the Salty River and met his arch-enemy, Professor Popcorn. He wanted to give the fruit to his Poppet Army and take over the Mingols. Leobro wasn't getting any of that drama. He flapped his wings and pushed the Poppet into a bush! Up! Up! Leobro went to the top of the mountain, where the fruit was planted. He harvested the fruits, flew back and gave them to the chicks.

Emily Woodward (10)
Loddiswell Primary School, Loddiswell

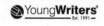

Super Alien

Once there was an alien called John who wanted to be a superhero. But other aliens didn't like him because he had eight legs instead of seven. He was determined to show them what he could do. One day, a bad alien stole the prince's coat. John spotted the bad alien, flicked his rocket boots to 'blast', and stopped him. John set off to the prince's palace to return the coat. He hid from the guards and hung the coat on the door. The prince saw him and gave him rewards. He truly was a superhero!

Liberty Motson (10)

Loddiswell Primary School, Loddiswell

The Big Chicken Was A Ball For Twenty-Five Years

Once upon a time, there was a chicken called Big Chick. Big Chick played rugby for England. He also scored in the Rugby World Cup final at the last second.

The game was against Ireland and the score was 23-22 to England. After they scored an enormous rugby ball appeared. Someone kicked it at Big Chick, so he became a rugby ball and by the time he was forty-five, the rugby ball had deflated. He popped out of it, but there was one last problem. He became a big yellow chicken but loved his life.

Archie Ball (11)
Loddiswell Primary School, Loddiswell

75

Titanic Mess

Once upon a time, in 1912, the Titanic set sail. The day flew past as they were sailing to New York. But they had struck an iceberg! Bob, a small monster, jumped on and no one saw because he put everyone to sleep and it sank! Bob was never popular and he wanted revenge so he thought the time had simply come to be a real monster! But when he told everyone they ignored him. He then felt bad so he went back in time and fixed it. So the Titanic didn't sink and he wanted to not be naughty.

Theo Cater (10)

Loddiswell Primary School, Loddiswell

The Lonely Monster

Once upon a time, there was a monster called Frederick and he was lonely. Very lonely indeed. So, one of his friends came to see him. She asked why he was sad. He said, "People have been bullying me."

His friend, Georgina, came and said, "When we get to school, I will tell the teacher, okay?"

"Okay then, but she might not believe me, so let's maybe tell her tomorrow," said Frederick. It was also his first day at school and he didn't know what people would say about him. "I'm afraid," said Frederick.

"So am I!"

Harry Vickers (7)
Metheringham Primary School, Metheringham

Alien Madness!

When Shifter got banned from Planet Budge he fell to Earth. He met someone called Jeff. They got to know each other and now they are friends.

One day Jeff and Shifter were on a walk when they saw a UFO. The UFO had crystals around it. The aliens said, "If someone doesn't break these crystals in thirty minutes then we will destroy this planet."

The pair rushed over and Shifter turned into a big hammer. The alien fired lasers at them but missed. They smashed all the crystals and made the aliens go back to their planet.

They saved everyone!

Thomas Creasey (9)

Metheringham Primary School, Metheringham

Bogo Ruins The City

He was still going - getting bigger every second, ruining everything in his sight. *Stomp, stomp. Chomp, chomp, chomp.* People tried to fight him but didn't succeed. Soon he (Bogo) would be the size of the moon! He'd eat the planet! That is if we didn't stop him soon. But together we could do this and stop Bogo from ruining the whole planet and all the wonderful things on it. After five minutes of thinking, we put together... the best ever army and managed to defeat him.

"Okay, bedtime now," said Mum.

Annabelle Washington (9)
Metheringham Primary School, Metheringham

Red's Victory

On the Rocky Planet, Red was bored. He entered the fish-shaped spaceship, but Red crashed on Minotaur Land. When he was falling down, he landed right in front of the Minotaur King. Then, Red smashed the sand timer to bits of glass. Afterwards, when the king was dead, all of the Minotaurs were dead. Five minutes later, Red was rewarded by the leader of the Gaming Planet. The reward was a pipe. Red put on his cow disguise and jumped in. When he fell out, he faked his death. Then, when nobody was looking, he played on a Nintendo Switch.

Hugh Herring (8)
Metheringham Primary School, Metheringham

The Explosion

One day, a little girl saw a tiny blob of goo at the park. She leaned over to touch it, but when she touched it, it exploded into ash. She did not know that was going to happen, but it did not get destroyed; it turned into a giant monster. She named it Gobble, and then they became friends. The monster did not know its parents, so it lived on its own, until it was touched. The girl decided to keep it. She brought it to school, but no one else could see it. Her parents didn't know, ever.

Cleo Newell (7)
Metheringham Primary School, Metheringham

81

Untitled

Once upon a time, on the coast of Spain, there lived a bird called Pink Venom. She once lived on a street called Alfred Avenue. But then, there was a flood, so she moved to England, to Metheringham, to see her friends and family. When she got to England, one of her friends died. On the day she got there, she found out that one of her friends had a baby. The baby was so cute and cuddly and pretty, you could not stop cuddling her. She was a dark blue, scary alien.

Roseanne Saffin (8)

Metheringham Primary School, Metheringham

Devi The Lost Princess

One day a beautiful princess was born, but a devastating discovery was found. The princess had been kidnapped. The king and queen were sad.
As the princess grew older everyone realised that she was different. She was bullied and cried every night. She never knew her mother, she was always disguised.
When Devi went out, her friend Harmony said, "I don't think that's your mum."
She researched. "You're the mythical princess!" screamed Harmony.
"Shh!" said Devi.
Devi ran to the castle. She faced challenges with fire and creatures.
Finally, she found the king and queen.
They're now very happy altogether.

Emma Donaldson (9)
Monymusk School, Monymusk

The Cyber Fight

"Bye, guys! That was fun," said Cyber Monkey.
"Bye!" said his friends. Cyber Monkey walked away,
but then Cyber Cat hit Cyber Monkey.
"Ow!" screamed Cyber Monkey in pain. Cyber
Monkey's friends came running over, and they took
Cyber Cat away. But then it happened again and
again, until one day he struck back, and they had a
fight. Cyber Monkey used his lasers, and Cyber Cat
moved out of the way, but Cyber Monkey did it
again. This time he hit Cyber Cat, and Cyber Cat
ran away and never did it again because he was
really, really scared.

Nathan Houston (10)
Monymusk School, Monymusk

The End

At the start of the world, there were slugs. Some had wings, some had arms and their names were Slug1, Slug2, Slug3 and so on.
Their queen was called Killer Queen and she had defended the continent. The tribe's enemy was End Dragon, for it had killed 2,003 slugs and, if Killer Queen did not defend, many, many more would be dead.
One day, Killer Queen went off to kill End Dragon! Killer Queen went into the cave. There was End Dragon.
Killer Queen charged at the dragon and stabbed her horn through its heart.

Lewis Gourley (9)
Monymusk School, Monymusk

Blobo And Blobh

Once upon a time, there was a Blob. His name was Blobo. He had an evil brother called Blobh. They lived in a city called Blobland. He teleported to New York to take over and rule the land. Blobh froze the Mayor and the whole town. All hope was lost until... Blobo! And, *boom!* He was captured... or so Blobo thought. Blobh had escaped. Blobo was so annoyed, so he shapeshifted into Blobh and he captured the real Blobh. He unfroze the Mayor and the town was freed once and for all.

Erin Wood (9)
Monymusk School, Monymusk

New World

One day, a monster was at a school. He had bad friends, and then a giant came to their school, and he crushed it! The monster was called Bobby. He said he wanted to go to a different world far away! It was big and scary and dark. He went into a house, the lights were off... A big flash hit the house! Bobby got scared; he went upstairs and went into a bedroom. Something was sleeping in the bed... He hid in the cupboard. A dog came into the room and woke what was in the bed.

Aubrey Miceal (8)
Monymusk School, Monymusk

Gem's Adventure

Once upon a time, I was outside at night, I saw a monster and it had red eyes. It started to chase me, and it ran past a tree! It crawled through the tree and got stuck halfway through. Its head was split open, and red slime burst out of its neck. Suddenly, I saw his head glue itself back together! It continued to chase me. I didn't know if I would get away. I ran into a tree; I didn't know if it would take me.

Josh Musselwhite (8)
Monymusk School, Monymusk

Shea's Adventure

My crazy creature is called Shea. Shea is half dog and half goat. Shea lives in a small cottage. Shea lives in a nice house. One day, Shea's enemy appeared. His name is Ripjaw. He has wings, and his wings are massive. He destroyed Shea's house. Shea used his laser eyes on Ripjaw. It was so powerful he got blasted back to jail. Shea and his mum and dad rebuilt the cottage. In one year, the cottage was done.

Jude McKenzie (9)
Monymusk School, Monymusk

89

Tomato Vs Carrots

One day, there was a tomato called Tomatay. He went to war to save Tomato Land. He was fighting really well, but then they ran out of bullets. No one else wanted to go, so Tomatay had to. He ran to the store next to him. He got the bullets and ran back. Everyone had bullets again. Then, they went on and won the war. Tomatay saved the town.

Jacob Field (9)
Monymusk School, Monymusk

Electric Mischief

Strolling through an empty field, Moonlight saw a little dragon coming her way. "Friend?" squeaked Floofy.

"Yes!" reported Moon.

"Electric?" screeched Floofy.

"Yes," reported Moon. Moon changed herself, but suddenly she ran out of Electric shots.

"Uh oh," shouted Floofy and Moon.

Floofy said to Moonlight, "Me, take you to the Electric realm!"

"Really?" said Moon, politely.

"Yes," screeched Floofy.

Floofy teleported her and Moonlight to the Electric realm. Moon changed herself and her abilities.

"Thank you so much!" shouted Moon.

"No problem, it's my thing, to save random friendly people!" squeaked Floofy, loudly.

"Oh!" shouted Moon.

Halle Pardoe (9)
Ryedene Primary & Nursery School, Vange

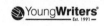

First Friend Forever?

Frightened and sweaty, Elecwire uneasily arose to an intruder in her crystal cave. The clock struck 4pm.

"Hiya, w-wanna be friends?" Elecwire grinned at a girl named Tasha, who had vitiligo.

She swiftly agreed.

Snapping her fingers, Elecwire teleported them to the Skiing Centre in the Skiiniverse! She drank hot chocolate in a Tuvoxees mug and gulped down her red velvet cupcake. *Yum!*

Battery low!

Gripping Tasha's cold, frosty hand, Elecwire teleported to her realm, Elecfire. "Why are we... here?" asked Tasha, uncomfortable.

"This is the charging port. You are human, so go there! Bye-bye," chuckled Elecwire.

"Bye?"

Elecwire disintegrated into dust.

Abigail Ncube (9)
Ryedene Primary & Nursery School, Vange

The Monster Theory

Quickly, injured Izzie woke up and took a deep breath. She ran and tumbled down the stairs and everyone froze. "They're playing musical statues without me," exclaimed Izzie. So she snapped her fingers calling the cat closer, and everyone unfroze. "Did I just discover my power?" she shouted. "Well, I shall head to Monstervania Centre." Then she started singing, "I'm so excited," while walking. So she was there at last where everyone was training their mesmerising powers. She breathed and pulled a giant joke on Big Burt! "Someone froze us!" Burt shouted.
"Me," Izzie exclaimed.

Evie Knight (10)
Ryedene Primary & Nursery School, Vange

93

Gearzo's Charge

Gearzo opened his robotic eye, staring at his battery. He cried out, "99%. I have to recharge or I'll run out." Running as fast as he could, he raced to the power charger system. Plugging himself into ultrasonic charging, he closed his eyes ready for charging.

"100%, fully charged, time to unplug," stated the employee.

But wait, something was happening, a warning showed 10%. He shut down overload! He had only heard stories about overload, something about eternal dreams. Planet Earth, year 19000, full of cars and machines. He had appeared in England. "What is this place?" asked Gearzo really confused.

Tommy Smith (10)
Ryedene Primary & Nursery School, Vange

Butterflysing Vs Evil Rainbow

In a magical, mysterious world lived Butterflysing, with sparkling clear fairy wings. Butterflysing loves going to Music School to express her feelings to everyone.

In Music Land, Butterflysing was shamed for having four eyes and being lazy. The unhappy, worried Butterflysing left Music Land and walked to Banana Land. She walked on a rainbow. Suddenly, she fell into a sticky, slimy pool. Scrambling for help, she had an idea, she shape-shifted to get out, and turned the evil rainbow into a happy rainbow, which flew into the clouds to reunite with his friends. Butterflysing jumped with excitement and saved Music Land from evil forever.

Munachi Udorji (10)
Ryedene Primary & Nursery School, Vange

Saving A Boy

Clang! Their heads bumped into one another.
"Emergency! Emergency!" the alarm screeched
through the speakers.
In a dash, Camo Calev rushed to the suck machine.
As Camo Calev exited the suck machine, he
thought to himself, *I wonder what the problem is?*
At that moment, he heard something.
Beep! Beep! Beep! A construction site.
Camo Calev, with his camouflage skin, tiptoed
through the colossal, green grass. Looking up, he
saw a boy in an old home, which was about to be
knocked down.
"Raaaaa!" Calev roared. The men ran, abandoning
the construction site; he had saved the day!

Archie Victory (9)
Ryedene Primary & Nursery School, Vange

Rampage At The Circus

Half asleep, Emily walked to the fridge; however, instead of a cake there was a sleeping creature. Using all six tentacles, it stood up. Thinking her mind was playing tricks on her, she continued her day at the circus with Fluff (the creature) following her.

At the circus, Fluff nearly strangled an elephant! This ended up with Fluff causing massive havoc. Everyone ran around like headless chickens! Suddenly, Aunt Ellan came with her creature. *Poof! Pow!*

The creature hovered around the circus and not a second later, Emily woke up in bed.

Maybe it was a dream or maybe it was not...

Hollie Che (10)
Ryedene Primary & Nursery School, Vange

97

A Big Fight

In a galaxy far, far away, there was a little scared boy. He worried about vampires, day and night. So one day, Marshmallow Millie the vampire decided to show him that there was nothing to be afraid of. *Crash!* Campfire Carrot entered. "Step away from Millie, petite boy!" shouted Carrot.

He did as he was told. Millie and Carrot had been enemies since they were little, so they burst into a fierce battle.

"Stop!" shouted the boy, as he froze everything and everyone, except Millie and Campfire Carrot. He talked to them and told them they had no reason to fight.

Taylor-Grace Stare (9)
Ryedene Primary & Nursery School, Vange

The Rumbler

I was walking calmly across a granite-hinged pathway and out of thin air, the ground started to rumble. It had stopped shaking and started again, it was continuous for five minutes. Suddenly, it continued, but a whole lot worse. *Bash! Thud! Crash!* A top-hatted monster flew out of the ground and landed centimetres away from me. I worryingly stood so still, it was like Medusa had just looked me in the eyes. Weirdly, it had begun circling me. For the next ten minutes, this unusual act went onwards. *Whoosh! Rumble!* It went back into the ground and happily went away.

Logan Painter (9)
Ryedene Primary & Nursery School, Vange

The Nightmare

One evening, a monster called Midnight just ate dinner, and then she went to bed. When she fell asleep a few hours later, she started to walk. After she hopped back in her bed, she felt a lick on her face. Suddenly, a bad dream formed; she was looking for a cafe called Yum Yum. She saw her enemies, ET and Sea, but not just one; she saw one thousand! She started to ruin the city, and everyone screamed. All of a sudden, her mum shouted loudly, "We're going to be late for our flight!"

"Okay, I'm just packing my suitcase," she replied.

Layla Hyde (10)
Ryedene Primary & Nursery School, Vange

Rudeysparkle Vs Snacknack's Final Boxing Creature Match

In Laindon, Rudeysparkle, a creature with two personalities, visited his local playground. He saw his enemies, Idonthavabrain# and Spockhi. Both sides hated them. He had turned off both sides and went to the nice side. He made a house called Junction 51 and lived there thinking he had run away from his enemies. He loved a playground called Funnymert. He laughed his lungs out. As he looked up, there were two bullies called Fairypolly and Bictik. He was scared on the nice side, but he switched to the bad side and slide-tackled both of them, at the same time!

Millie Pope (9)
Ryedene Primary & Nursery School, Vange

What Happens At Night

This is Darkness and I'm going to tell you all about him. Most people are terrified of him but he's not that bad. Let me tell you what he does. He used to be the coolest around, he would take people's dreams and make them more positive. One time, after midnight, he snatched a boy named Billy's dreams and tried to make them positive, but his dreams were peculiar. They were shrouded with negativity. It made him crazy! He and Morning made a deal that after midnight he could take people's dreams, but after, he has to be long gone!

Timmy Ganiyu (10)
Ryedene Primary & Nursery School, Vange

The Saddest Monster In The World

Yawning, Dream Maker got out of bed to shop. Everyone was mean to him because he was different. So he left Dream Village for Earth. While on Earth Joe, who is ten years old, found Dream Maker. They played football and Fortnite together. The Parliament found out. So they sent scientists to capture the monster. While sleeping the scientists captured him to study his DNA. When Dream Maker woke up he knew he was never going to see Joe again. When Joe woke up he was devastated he'd lost his best friend and they never saw each other again.

Jayden Roberts (10)
Ryedene Primary & Nursery School, Vange

The Sad Origin Story Of Jim

One day, a monster named Jim moved away from the town of Jimaica, all the way to Orlando. He missed his family and friends a lot; he was so upset he hid from everyone for two weeks.

Out of nowhere, Jim concentrated hard. He knew, if he put his mind to forgetting everyone, they would turn into coal... *Boom!*

Later that day, he came out for some fresh air and to see if it had worked. It had... worked! But he realised something was wrong. He was alone.

He was sad. He needed to figure out how to turn everyone back.

Scarlett Pearce (10)

Ryedene Primary & Nursery School, Vange

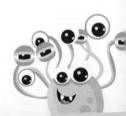

The Strawberry Ice Cream Thief

One morning, I woke up at half-five to the sound of my freezer opening slowly. I crept downstairs to the kitchen to see a bat-like creature going through my freezer! Suddenly, it stared at me wondering why I was there. The creature had my strawberry ice cream and was eating it all up. I walked over to the small window to let it go, since I had school soon and Mum couldn't find out. Unfortunately, the creature stayed put which was a problem. I gave up and decided to sit down. All of a sudden, Mum silently came downstairs...

Bella Roberts (10)
Ryedene Primary & Nursery School, Vange

The Crazy Sparkle Against The Annoying Statue

One hot, dry day, Sparkle, who lived in Candyland, walked down the street to pick some candy. Suddenly, it got really cold and wet, and it was time to go to bed.

That night, she heard a strange sound. She ignored it. As the sun rose, Sparkle awoke and she was getting hungry.

She went out and walked through the trees to go to the chocolate fountain. Spotting a statue in front of it, she made a plan. Her plan was to trap the statue in a pot.

She put candy in the pot, then she trapped it and lived happily ever after.

Layla Guzel (9)

Ryedene Primary & Nursery School, Vange

When The Gunk Attacked

Sally wakes up and there is a big lump of gunk on her floor. She thinks nothing of it but when she walks out of her house, half the floor is gunk! People are covered. Sally goes down to a shop, but there is no cashier, so Sally gets a chocolate for free. Sally goes down to Fred's Fish 'n' Chips and gets a large chip for free. Woo hoo! Best day ever, until she falls down into a lump of gunk. Her alarm clock rings.
"Time for school!" shouted Mum. Turns out the whole thing was just a bad dream.

Brodie Loveday (10)
Ryedene Primary & Nursery School, Vange

The Evil Splinter

Spotty has just woken up but hears a strange knock on the door. He goes downstairs to see a letter at the door. The letter is opened. It isn't a letter, it is an invitation. He is so excited for the party. In the news it says there is a new clothing shop down the road. He goes upstairs and changes. The shop closes at four so he sprints as fast as a cheetah to the shops. He finds some clothes and buys them. He sprints home to try them on.

The day of the party arrives and... "Owww, a splinter!"

Marshall Dell-Murphy (10)

Ryedene Primary & Nursery School, Vange

The Comeback

At school, three bullies bully Fourarms. Their names are Jim, Tim and Fred. They beat him up and find out he has black blood. He gets mad and turns into a creature.

They run for hours and hide. There is silence. Then Fourarms is above Jim, Tim and Fred, but they don't know.

He jumps down and taps one of their shoulders. They all sprint away. Then Jim, Tim and Fred beat Fourarms up again.

He runs home and gets his friends. The bullies ask him to fight them again and he wins.

Reagan Williams Cooper (10)
Ryedene Primary & Nursery School, Vange

All About The Crazy Clown

Crazy Clown woke up in the night. He saw everyone was asleep. "It is my chance," whispered the clown as he went down the stairs. He knocked on his friend's door, waiting patiently until his enemy came out. He knocked on the wrong door and started running away! He went to a carnival and jumped on an elephant, showing all of his tricks, but then, the elephant took him down, and everyone ran away. The police came, and he jumped down a drain to get home.

Meadow Dowson (9)

Ryedene Primary & Nursery School, Vange

Scull The Monster

One night I was walking home from the shop. I heard something behind me. I looked, but nothing was there. I started walking again. I got home and, before you knew it, I opened the door. I heard it again and looked. Nothing there. I went up the stairs and started watching my phone. I heard it again, but this time I saw it. It was cute but scary. It disappeared. It was chasing me downstairs, then it went invisible. It chased me right into the kitchen. Turns out it was just hungry!
I said, "Are you hungry?"
"Yes."
"Okay, follow me."

Sophie Truesdale (10)
Shawhead Primary School, Shawhead

111

Blob's Battle

Blob was peacefully sitting on his comfy couch when Splat his enemy messaged him and told Blob he wanted to battle. Blob obviously said yes. They planned the fight and decided it was on Silent Sun. Blob then called his friend Angry Allan. The next day they went to Silent Sun and were ready to battle. Mid-battle when Blob was losing Angry Allan came over and helped Blob. They were both using their powers and Splat was losing. Blob was happy and Splat tapped out. But when Blob was sitting on his couch he got a message that said 'Rematch?'

Katie Cockburn (12)
Shawhead Primary School, Shawhead

Katrina Rubber Saves The World

One night, Katrina Rubber and Mr Whiteboard were in their secret hideout when they saw Dr Swizzles out of the corner of their eyes. He had a ray to take over the world.

They jumped out of their secret hideout to capture him. They climbed up the houses to get the ray. They did so and then they put him in jail. Then they decided to invite everyone and celebrate, but the villain in jail had a mission to break out.

They were partying when, all of a sudden, they got an email saying the prisoner had finally broken out...

Sophie-Mae Johnstone (10)
Shawhead Primary School, Shawhead

Tentacle Man

Tentacle Man is an old mystical creature who enters children's minds when they sleep. Tentacle Man has got ten tentacles, two heads and is very fast and strong. Tentacle Man is only bad so that he can turn bad children into good ones. He enters all around the world.

Many children have mentioned to their parents about this strange creature, waking up every morning a changed little boy or girl who was bad and now turned good. Parents all over the world have thanked Tentacle.

Angela Slavin (10)
Shawhead Primary School, Shawhead

Element Monster

One day in a world of monsters, there was a monster named Element Monster. He was very good at making elements and giving people elements as well. He met something and it gave him a mission to stop a bully from taking out the world. It was a building that could talk, and the Element Monster started making elements. He found the person and gave him the elements. It was a hard fight but the monster won against the bully. Then the Element Monster and the person became friends.

Sammie Sharp (11)
Shawhead Primary School, Shawhead

115

I'm Not Like Other Monsters!

The girl crept inside the haunted house that she'd heard about from the people of Hauntville.

"Alo!" a friendly, scary-looking monster greeted her cheerfully.

"Ahh!" the girl screamed, and suddenly everything went black.

Eventually, after a long, boring hour, the girl gasped and woke up to see a kind creature smiling. The girl told herself not to worry. She gave Monsme (the creature) a smile.

"Can we be friends?" Monsme sounded like a baby.

The girl agreed, but went home because it was getting dark. She promised Monsme that she would meet her after school, so they became best friends forever after.

Rida Fatima (11)
St Clare's Catholic Primary School, Handsworth

Zigaline's Act Of Courage

Zigaline, who was from the Planet of Nature, arrived inside the substantial, distasteful school. She had left her beloved planet just to be in an obscure atmosphere where no one seemed to care about her.

"You look so grotesque," exclaimed a scruffy-looking boy as she shrank away in embarrassment. Zigaline felt like she was being disrespected for her peculiar appearance.

She mustered up her courage and stated, "You have no right to disrespect me and you should treat me with dignity." The boy's face was one of guilt as his mouth endeavoured to open. Zigaline understood and beamed.

Fedora Nkrumah (10)
St Clare's Catholic Primary School, Handsworth

From Nightmares To Dreams

One day, Dreaming Seline was watching children, keeping them from nightmares. Until, a person called Nightmare Tom swooped into a little girl's dreams and corrupted them with nightmares. "Oh no! I need to save her!" Dreaming Seline rushed from Planet Garp to Earth to save the little girl. Dreaming Seline went inside the girl's mind, and there she found Nightmare Tom. They started fighting and Dreaming Seline managed to beat Nightmare Tom and restore the little girl's dreams. Then Dreaming Seline went back to Planet Garp with a smile on her big face. Another dream had been restored.

Seim Teklesenbet (10)
St Clare's Catholic Primary School, Handsworth

Dreamer-Dan

In the middle of hibernation, the dreamers suddenly got an alert. Yawning and whispering erupted suddenly in space. After minutes of silence, Dreamer-Dan spoke. "I'll go." It was agreed and they fuelled his wings with special dust to fight the nightmares. Dan arrived quite a bit after Nightmare Nick with the dust in his wings. Dan dashed past Nick and his wings just managed to fly past him unseen. The remains of Nick's spotted body were scattered and carefully with his sticky pads, Dan collected the remains and used his antenna to remove the bad energy. Mission completed!

Goodness Nlemoha (10)
St Clare's Catholic Primary School, Handsworth

119

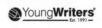

The Walk Through The Park

On Planet Earth, a young boy walked through the park during the night. He looked up at the sky. It was a spaceship! "Does that mean aliens exist?" whispered the boy. "Surely they can't exist. I refuse to believe so."

"Well, you're wrong boy," added Roy as he landed on Planet Earth.

"W-w-who are you?" said the boy, frightened.

"I am Roy," said the alien loudly. "I am from Planet Plumars and now I will demolish you!"

"Ahh!" screamed the boy. "It must've been a nightmare, right?"

Nazakat Hussain (10)

St Clare's Catholic Primary School, Handsworth

Hairy Heapy-Hope

One sunny afternoon, in sandy Spain, a little girl named Tina sat all alone, sad and fearful. She was too scared of Goolians and had no friends. Out of nowhere came Hairy Heapy-Hope from The Magic Island in Arizona. He fought the Goolians and tickled Tina with his hairy hand. Heapy-Hope defeated the Goolians with the boingy antenna and hairy hands, who were gone forever. He created a play area filled with toys and rides for the children of Tina's age, attracting many children. Eventually, Tina's life was filled with joy and fun without any fear.

Alayna-Jannah Adam (11)
St Clare's Catholic Primary School, Handsworth

Lilly Is Captured

A long time ago there lived an animal. The animal was called a cat-dragon, Lilly. She lived on Pluto. A long time passed, but one day, the astronauts came to Planet Pluto. The cat-dragon was scared, but suddenly, the astronauts broke in and captured her. She was placed in a cage. She was so scared and worried thinking about a miserable life on Earth. Suddenly she thought about Pluto. So she broke out and freed her planet from destruction. The astronauts were never to be seen on Planet Pluto ever again. She was happy that was over. She was relieved.

Ameera Hussain (9)
St Clare's Catholic Primary School, Handsworth

The Lonely Shapeshifting Giant

Once upon a time, upon the mountains in the ancient village of Petra, there lived a lonely giant. One day, the giant became very bored and decided to use his shapeshifting powers to turn into a human.

He went down into the village. When he entered, nobody questioned him. He lived in the village for a few days.

One day, the king said they were going to do a census. When they finished, the king noticed that they had an extra person. Because the king was very cautious, the person (who was the giant) was kicked out.

Joan Chinedu (11)
St Clare's Catholic Primary School, Handsworth

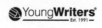
The Five-Eyed Dragon And His Children

One day, a dragon went hunting. While he was setting a trap, he heard a strange sound. Cautiously and bravely, he walked closer to where the sound was coming from.

To his surprise, he saw a fox trapped in a net. He tried to eat it, but it was a fake fox. It was a trap, and he got captured.

His children were at home, pacing around worriedly. They went out to the woods to find their father, but they faced so many obstacles. The main obstacle was that animals attacked them, but they were able to find their father.

Jessica Chinedu (10)
St Clare's Catholic Primary School, Handsworth

A Trip To Earth!

Once upon a time, a spaceship was called to Earth. A little girl was being attacked by aliens! They had to save her! But what to do? They flew to Earth and searched for her house. They found it! Then they barged into her house. They found her... but it was too late. The alien bit her with the venom from its fangs. Fireball saw Nightfang and looked at him with squinted eyes.

"This is not over!"

Fireball leapt at him, but he missed. Nightfang flew out into the darkness and he was never seen again.

Ameera Jannat Ali (10)
St Clare's Catholic Primary School, Handsworth

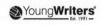
The Beautiful Mermaid

Once upon a time, there lived a princess with her family of mermaids. She was the most beautiful girl in the kingdom and because of that, her parents decided to sell her for money. The kingdom next to theirs was looking for a bride for their son in exchange for a lot of gold. On the day of their wedding, the princess overheard the king and queen saying that they were going to kill her. The princess, being so clever, decided to sneak out. As she was about to leave, she was caught and thrown in jail.

Joan Chinedu (11)
St Clare's Catholic Primary School, Handsworth

Dragonfly

There was once a girl called Lia. She was playing a game on Roblox when it happened. The game she was playing was called Animal Roleplay, her character was a dragonfly called Rae. But things for Lia changed. All of a sudden, she pressed a button that read 'Game Life'. Immediately Lia was knocked out cold, but when she woke Lia found herself resting on a gargantuan daisy flower. And when she realised she was trapped, Lia decided to try and help the other animals. But, when she tried to help a tiger things took a dramatic turn...

Ella Haggerty (10)
St John's Catholic Junior School, Bebington

Untitled

On Earth, a little girl waited for her monster to come and fix her worries. The monster always dreamed of helping a little one but it was always his older brother, Sith, who got all the attention. But he went to the mood centre and begged to be sent to fix a little one's mood. They said fine, and he was off to the teleportation room. He got there and he was talking to her about her feelings, she was delighted he sorted her feelings. He had to go back to Planet Mood May. They said bye and he left.

Sophia Reynolds (10)
St John's Catholic Junior School, Bebington

Planet Big Bin

On Big Bin there is a crazy, stinky creature called Bob 2001. Bob said he wanted you to know about him. So he is short, hairy, naughty, spotty, big-mouthed, fluffy, clever and, most definitely, *stinky*. Bob has one enemy who is... Jimmy the Yeti. He steals all of Bob's bins but yesterday Bob stole all of his bins back. Job done but wait, Bob has not done his special move which is a dumpster dive. "Woooohooo!" says Bob.

Evie Pettersson (9)
St John's Catholic Junior School, Bebington

Mike And The Slitherbeast

Once upon a time, there was a boy named Mike. Mike lived in a village called Marvellia. There was one problem. Mike had a dream to venture into Adventure Forest and kill a monster called Slitherbeast. The Slitherbeast stole Mike's brother when he was young and Mike wanted revenge. So he ran away from home and into the Slitherbeast's lair. Then Mike and the Slitherbeast had an epic battle that lasted four days. On the last day, Mike chopped off the Slitherbeast's head and got back his brother. Mike and his brother sold the head and lived happily ever after.

Ray Johnson (11)
St Mary's Catholic Primary School, Bognor Regis

Giggle Feelings

An alien called Giggle-goal leaves his precious planet because he believes that everyone doesn't like him. When he scores and does his celebration, they laugh because he creates a silly, different dance every time he scores. He lands on Earth whilst fleeing from Planet Sport and injures himself. He is brought to a government hospital, so they can identify what he is. After being in a coma, Giggle wakes up to the sight of his doctors laughing at a joke one of them has said. He then realises that his neighbours aren't giggling at him but instead, with him.

Benjamin Dlugaszek (10)
St Mary's Catholic Primary School, Bognor Regis

Defeat Of A Giant

Daniela the five-eyed dragon was practising her karate. Her post dropped through the letterbox and there was a letter asking her to go to the Las Vegas strip for a karate competition against her nemesis the Giant Ant. So, a week later Daniela was preparing for the competition. She was a short friendly girl and was scared of the Giant Ant in front of her glaring menacingly. It wasn't going well but everyone started cheering her name. With a tornado kick the Giant Ant was down.
Always have self-belief and you will be a winner like Daniela the dragon.

Izzy Skeef (11)
St Mary's Catholic Primary School, Bognor Regis

Blaze And The Fire-Breathing Creature Ferns

Once upon a time, there was a monster called Blaze. His family died at a young age. Blaze went flying around in his spaceship, helping people in need. But Ferno kept causing trouble, so Blaze challenged him to a fight. Blaze hit the first punch, but soon after, Ferno followed with a face-smashing punch. *Pow! Bang! Crash!* But Blaze got up and flew with his wings in the air. He came down with a mighty force. Down went Ferno. Blaze was praised by everyone because he saved them. Blaze flew away in his spaceship. Now he saves people every day.

Lucas Law (10)
St Mary's Catholic Primary School, Bognor Regis

Bobby Makes Friends

Bobby was just chilling in the sun until there was a huge crash! Bobby was worried, so he peeked around the corner and a huge rocket ship appeared on Bobby's planet. At first, Bobby thought that this was one of his, but instead of a monster, it was something else, someone with two feet, two hands and two eyes. So Bobby did what he had to do, he went up to the man and Bobby realised that humans aren't scary at all.
So Bobby said, "Do you want to be friends?"
The man replied, "Yes."

Lexi Hickey (7)
St Mary's Catholic Primary School, Bognor Regis

Jan And Sultart

Once upon a time, there was a boy called Jan (me), who found a mysterious little person, so he adopted him. One day, Jan and Sultart went to the supermarket and he got lost. He looked everywhere, but there was no sign, so he decided to spend the night at the supermarket. During the sleep, his enemy, Ripper, crawled and got him. When he was awake he got into a fight. Sultart was strong so he fought Ripper and obviously, he won. He suddenly remembered his house. He got inside and saw Jan. Jan was so happy to see him.

Jan Spiewak (9)
St Mary's Catholic Primary School, Bognor Regis

Bob's Eventful Day Out

Once upon a time, in the land of Jequvius, there was a blob monster called Bob. After Bob got up he went to see his best friend, Kelvin. But as soon as he got there Kelvin had a petrified look on his face.

He stuttered, "Bob, he has come to kill us." After all, it was the monster blob named Killer.

"Listen up, Killer. We are united and we love each other."

After a while, the Killer started to tear up and exclaimed, "You're right. I shouldn't do this."

Florence Burles (9)

St Mary's Catholic Primary School, Bognor Regis

Bob Vs The Tea Shop

One day, Bob was embarking on a trip to a tea shop. He left his cup outside. When he returned, his cup had been stolen! Just then, he saw somebody run away with his cup, so he climbed on the wall and tripped with his cup. It smashed into pieces. But then, he remembered something! How did he turn into a puddle without his cup? Bob looked in his hand and saw his cup. The other person was in tears because his special cup had broken. Bob had to do something, so he gave his own cup to the man as an apology.

Merson Cooper (10)
St Mary's Catholic Primary School, Bognor Regis

137

The Lost Mermaid

A young mermaid, Lilly, was afraid and lost, unable to find her home. Pleading the fish for directions, she stumbled across a dark cave and entered. The exquisite mermaid thought to herself, *should I be in here and is anything dangerous?*
Lilly approached the end of the cave, she was starting to get nervous but as the brave, little mermaid she was, she carried on. *Stomp! Stomp! Stomp!* All of a sudden, an immense yeti, named Sooty, appeared from the darkness, claiming he knew the way home. The yeti led her home and she allowed him to stay. They became best friends.

Heidi Rumbold (10)
Thistle Hill Academy, Minster-On-Sea

The Story Of Plumbeast

On planet Unknown lived Plumbeast. His dream was to find a home. First, he travelled to Flat Bottom City where everyone laughed at him for his big bottom. He felt really rejected. Next, he flew to Middle Bottom City. He tried to make friends but they all said, "You don't belong here."
He ran to his ship crying because he didn't fit in. He then found Planet Peach, where whoever had the biggest bottom would be the king. Plumbeast entered the competition, he won the crown for the biggest bottom.
He is now the king and finally living happily ever after.

Kai Llufrio (9)
Thistle Hill Academy, Minster-On-Sea

A Teenage Dream

One day, there was a teenage girl called Molly and her dream was to go to Disneyland. But her family could never afford it, so Molly decided to stop trying to go and let her dream go. But soon, it was going to change. In her head, she heard a little voice saying, "Don't give up!" so Molly put her foot down, quit school and started a babysitting business for sixty pounds per session.

She did it for weeks and weeks until the day came when they finally went. They had so much fun as a family.

Ava-Sophia Monks (10)

Thistle Hill Academy, Minster-On-Sea

The Devil And Angel Shapeshifter

Once, the Devil Shapeshifter and the Angel Shapeshifter roamed Earth. One day, they went to war on Earth, killing thousands of humans. The Devil went to planet Oz and the Angel went to planet Zo. Next year, the Devil Shapeshifter called a truce. They shook hands but the Angel Shapeshifter smirked. He became a dragon and burned everything, After about five minutes, he was banished to lava.

"No!" he shrieked and he fell into the lava. Everyone cheered for the Devil Shapeshifter and all the humans celebrated. So the Devil Shapeshifter was now the Angel Shapeshifter.

Viktoria Limontaite (9)

Walpole Highway Primary School, Wisbech

The Elf

Once upon a time, there was an evil elf who wanted to destroy Santa's workshop. He clogged the teddy machine and ruined the sacks by gnawing them. The elf had naughty eyes and rows of razor-sharp teeth used for nibbling, "Christmas will be ruined," he giggled.

Santa heard the banging of machines, the teddies ripping and a creepy giggle. Santa got a titanium bag and tiptoed up to the naughty elf; a chase commenced. Finally, Santa grabbed him and locked him into a shiny box. Santa saved Christmas, and now, the elf only comes out to be on the shelf.

Charlie Saward (9)

Walpole Highway Primary School, Wisbech

The Coffee Monster Under Your Bed

Once upon a monster time, there was a monster that loved coffee. He hid under people's beds and scared them. He could make children dizzy in the head and scare them to death. One time he was under someone's bed, he came out and was caught like a prisoner in jail. The tiny small girl screamed like a siren. He got scared like a baby crying. The girl noticed and comforted him. They hung out all the time. But one day, the parents found out. They kicked him. He was left in the dark night. The little girl helped him.

Ciara Shinn (10)

Walpole Highway Primary School, Wisbech

The Story Of The Fight: Purple Burple Against Pinkie Winky

Once, there was a monster. His name was Purple Burple. He liked to burp, also he could shapeshift into a boy. Purple Burple lived on a planet called Planet Burple. Purple Burple wanted to help everywhere and anywhere. It was his time to shine. It was the day, he could finally help. Purple Burple flashed down when he saw his enemy, Pinky Winky! His brother! Purple Burple flashed down at the speed of light. He turned into a boy to investigate. He erased all of his bullies' brains to forget everything and the boy was not bullied ever again.

Holly Hill (10)
Walpole Highway Primary School, Wisbech

Planet Woofow!

Once, there was a cat girl called Zoe. She was an undercover spy and was about to be assigned a mission, but her enemy was assigned to be her partner. The enemy's name was Daisy. The mission was called Operation BFF, but Zoe and Daisy thought that it was called Operation Student Behave. Zoe and Daisy went to Earth and learned the true meaning of friendship. They stayed on Earth for a couple of months, returned to their planets, and convinced the two planets to be friends and not enemies, so they became BFFAEs and became Planet Woofow!

Emi Webb (10)
Walpole Highway Primary School, Wisbech

Clob And Logan

A little boy called Logan really needed a friend. Clob was a shapeshifter, he changed himself into a boy and became friends with Logan. They played board games together. One day Logan found out about Clob being a monster, but they decided to be friends anyway. Together they played lots of pranks and were mischievous because Clob could be any shape! One day Clob's enemy, Stinky Pants, tried to capture Logan, but luckily Clob saved the day and sent Stinky Pants to monster jail! Logan and Clob stayed friends forever.

Harry Saward (7)

Walpole Highway Primary School, Wisbech

Space Dump

Once, there was a big planet called Zootroom. It was a land of candy. In that land was a girl monster called Cassy. She loved to whistle and looked like an elephant with a fox tail.

One day, when Cassy went outside, it was a mess. She saw pillars of rubbish. Her planet was destroyed.

She went to the judge and asked to go and find where it came from. She went in her space rocket down to Earth. There she made a friend called Charlotte.

Cassy asked Charlotte to lend her a home and she said yes.

Araminta Chamberlain (9)

Walpole Highway Primary School, Wisbech

147

Crazy Kreep

He was born in the middle of space as a child. But because he was born in space, he suffocated, then turned into Crazy Kreep and was sent down to Earth.

On Earth, he went to school, and he was bullied for how small he was. When the children didn't finish their homework, they would go to the head teacher, then they realised that the head teacher was the small boy. When the children were really naughty, he would shapeshift into Crazy Kreep. When he was done with the children, he would haunt them.

Logan Lord (7)
Walpole Highway Primary School, Wisbech

The Skull Sorcerer

"You're a disgrace in our family," said Mom and Dad in anger.
"Sorry, I can't help it," said the Skull Sorcerer.
"You belong on Earth," said Dad.
So the Skull Sorcerer went in the rocket, started the engine, and blasted off. When he arrived on Earth, he had to face so many challenges. He stole supplies, fought the bad, and defeated his dad against destroying the world. Everyone cheered, he became rich and famous, and everyone loved him so much.

Albie Sadrija (9)
Walpole Highway Primary School, Wisbech

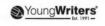

Noogy Loogy Strikes Again

There was once a spider who was born in the sky and was very scary. He started the day by going to a birthday party to eat teachers.

His favourite food to eat was teachers, so he ruined the kid's birthday party. Noogy Loogy was ready to leap on the teacher, but it was too late. They moved out of the way and he couldn't get his meal.

He was still hungry, so he went on another mission for food and, yet again, he leapt out and got his food.

He was now happy.

Mason Nicholls (9)
Walpole Highway Primary School, Wisbech

The Stalker

Once, on a foggy night, a mother and little girl were sitting across the road. They saw something, it came towards them. It had a white face with bright red eyes and a black coat, with half an arm. He reached out and gave them a key. He smiled. He offered them a lovely, wooden cabin to live in. The mother and girl were very excited. They walked and locked the door. The mother barricaded them inside.
He walked away, laughing. They were trapped forever!

Vinnie Webster (9)
Walpole Highway Primary School, Wisbech

Bill The Homework Thief

There once was a red scary monster that liked to eat homework. His name was Bill. Homework kept disappearing from the teacher's desk, it must be Bill!
The children loved it but the teachers didn't so they had a plan to catch the homework thief! The teachers waited until dark to catch him. They grabbed him in a net and took him in a net away to a different school to make sure he never returned. The teachers decided to never set homework ever again!

Bailey Hogg (8)
Walpole Highway Primary School, Wisbech

Eyeball Boy

Once, there was a green, slimy, slithery, sloppy monster. He was in Monster School and was playing, but suddenly, it went dark! His eyeballs had run away. He found a hoover in a dark cupboard. He turned it on and, *suck!* His eyeballs popped into the hoover. Eyeball Boy could put them back into his head, but they were all dusty. He took them out and gave them a sloppy lick. He was trying to get attention because he then was juggling with his eyes!

Billie Panks (8)
Walpole Highway Primary School, Wisbech

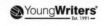

The Story Of The World Saver

On Planet Snal, he had to kill his mortal enemy, Predatorial. He searched for him and his sidekick, Bidmatic. To find him, he used a high-tech signal to locate him. He found him with a shock. He was already defeated, but he heard a ticking sound. It was a bomb.

Once he recovered, he set off to find him. He could've lost his job. He found him and finally defeated him. He got his bounty.

Flynn Roberts (9)

Walpole Highway Primary School, Wisbech

Buzz Finds A New Home

Buzz lives on the moon. He's blue and has many arms. He decides to visit Earth to explore.
He makes lots of friends, but he thinks they are aliens. They only have two arms!
He decides to live on Earth because he is lonely on the moon. His favourite thing on Earth is going to parties. He makes lots more friends.
Going somewhere new is the best thing you can do!

Taylor Hogg (8)
Walpole Highway Primary School, Wisbech

YOUNG WRITERS INFORMATION

We hope you have enjoyed reading this book – and that you will continue to in the coming years.

If you're a young writer who enjoys reading and creative writing, or the parent of an enthusiastic poet or story writer, do visit our website **www.youngwriters.co.uk**. Here you will find free competitions, workshops and games, as well as recommended reads, a poetry glossary and our blog.

If you would like to order further copies of this book, or any of our other titles, then please give us a call or visit **www.youngwriters.co.uk**.

Young Writers
Remus House
Coltsfoot Drive
Peterborough
PE2 9BF
(01733) 890066
info@youngwriters.co.uk

Scan me to watch the Crazy Creatures video!

f YoungWritersUK **X** YoungWritersCW

@ youngwriterscw **♪** youngwriterscw